Dear Parent:

Congratulations! Your child is taking the first steps on an exciting journey. The destination? Independent reading!

STEP INTO READING® will help your child get there. The program offers five steps to reading success. Each step includes fun stories and colorful art. There are also Step into Reading Sticker Books, Step into Reading Math Readers, Step into Reading Write-In Readers, Step into Reading Phonics Readers, and Step into Reading Phonics First Steps! Boxed Sets—a complete literacy program with something for every child.

Learning to Read, Step by Step!

Ready to Read Preschool–Kindergarten
• big type and easy words • rhyme and rhythm • picture clues
For children who know the alphabet and are eager to begin reading.

Reading with Help Preschool–Grade 1
• basic vocabulary • short sentences • simple stories
For children who recognize familiar words and sound out new words with help.

Reading on Your Own Grades 1–3
• engaging characters • easy-to-follow plots • popular topics
For children who are ready to read on their own.

Reading Paragraphs Grades 2–3
• challenging vocabulary • short paragraphs • exciting stories
For newly independent readers who read simple sentences with confidence.

Ready for Chapters Grades 2–4
• chapters • longer paragraphs • full-color art
For children who want to take the plunge into chapter books but still like colorful pictures.

STEP INTO READING® is designed to give every child a successful reading experience. The grade levels are only guides. Children can progress through the steps at their own speed, developing confidence in their reading, no matter what their grade.

Remember, a lifetime love of reading starts with a single step!

For A.M.B., keeper of dreams

Text copyright © 1984 by Harriet Ziefert. Illustrations copyright © 1984 by Norman Gorbaty, Inc. All rights reserved under International and Pan-American Copyright Conventions. Published in the United States by Random House Children's Books, a division of Random House, Inc., New York, and simultaneously in Canada by Random House of Canada Limited, Toronto.

www.stepintoreading.com

Educators and librarians, for a variety of teaching tools, visit us at www.randomhouse.com/teachers

Library of Congress Cataloging-in-Publication Data
Ziefert, Harriet.
Sleepy dog / by Harriet Ziefert ; illustrated by Norman Gorbaty. p. cm. SUMMARY: Simple text and illustrations portray a small dog getting ready for bed, sleeping, dreaming, and waking up.
ISBN 0-394-86877-3 (trade) — ISBN 0-394-96877-8 (lib. bdg.)
[1. Bedtime—Fiction. 2. Dreams—Fiction. 3. Night—Fiction. 4. Dogs—Fiction.]
I. Gorbaty, Norman, ill. II. Title. PZ7.Z487 Sl 2003 [E]—dc21 2002013650

Printed in the United States of America 70 69 68

STEP INTO READING, RANDOM HOUSE, and the Random House colophon are registered trademarks of Random House, Inc.

STEP INTO READING®

STEP 1

Sleepy Dog

by Harriet Ziefert

illustrated by Norman Gorbaty

Random House New York

Chapter 1: Sleepy Dog

"Time for bed,
sleepyhead."

Sleepy, sleepy,
up to bed.

Head on pillow.

Nose under covers.

Cat on bed.

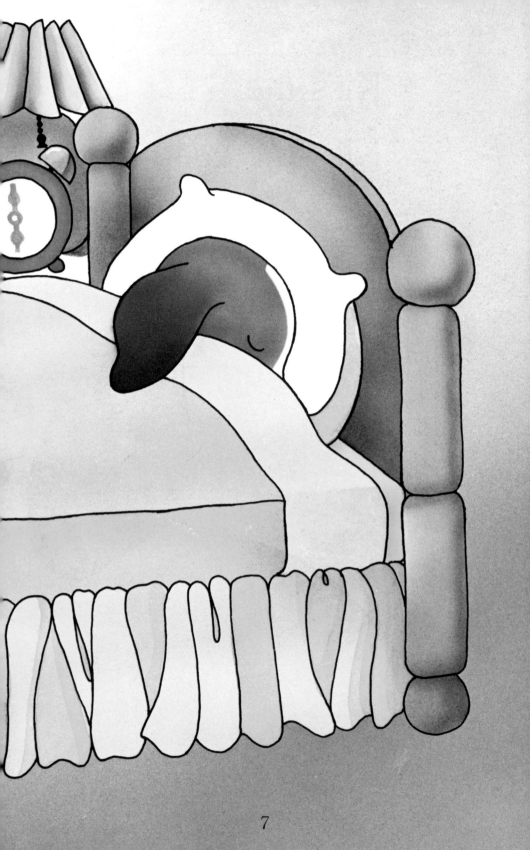

Kiss me.

Kiss me good.

Kiss me good night.

Turn on the moon.

Turn off the light.

Sleepy, sleepy,
sweet dreams tonight.

Chapter 2: Dreaming

I dream

I am eating.

I dream

I am jumping.

I dream

I am running.

Someone is chasing me. HELP!

Now I am awake.

I need a drink
of water.

Sleepy, sleepy,
back to bed.

Chapter 3: The Clock

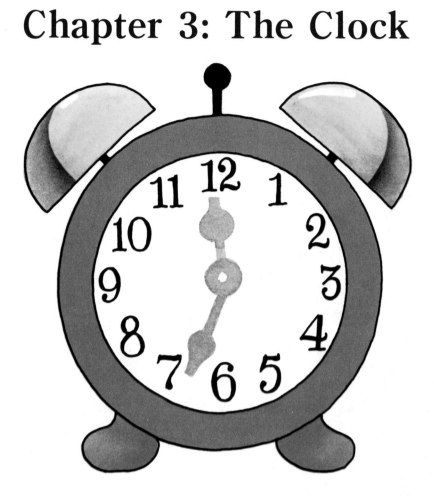

Tick, tick, tick, tick.

The clock says

tick, tick, tick, tick.

The clock shouts
ring, ring, ring!
Wake up!

Turn off the moon.

Turn off the clock.

Turn on the sun.

Turn on the light.

Good morning, cat...

time to play!

"Good morning,
little dog."